Teaching Squash

Teaching Squash

by

CLAIRE CHAPMAN

LONDON: G. BELL & SONS LTD

First published in 1976 by
G. Bell & Sons Ltd
York House, 6 Portugal Street
London WC2A 2HL

ISBN 0 7135 1951 7

Printed in Great Britain by
The Camelot Press Ltd, Southampton

Contents

Foreword

It is with pleasure that I write this Foreword to a squash book which has been long overdue. There have been many books written on how to play squash, but nobody has thought about writing a book on how to *teach* squash (a completely different approach is needed) and it is not before time that such a book now appears.

Claire Chapman's book should be included in any squash coach's library at whatever level he or she teaches the game. It gives a clear understanding of stroke technique and tactics but more important it highlights the essential requirements of a good lesson. It covers both individual and group coaching and I shall have no hesitation in recommending this book *Teaching Squash* to any candidates of mine who are training to become either coaches or fully qualified professionals. It will serve as a useful reference book for any SRA or WSRA coaching course, at the elementary or advanced level, and I would like to wish Claire Chapman every success with this her first book and commend it to you.

ANTHONY SWIFT
Senior National Coach
Squash Rackets Association
July 1975

Acknowledgments

During many years as a player, coach and official of the game, I have been helped by countless people and am particularly indebted to Mrs. A. Shardlow, M.B.E. (Janet Morgan) whose knowledge of the game and ability to play it are second to none.

I have Tony Chapman to thank for taking the photographs, Philip Ayton for appearing in them and Coolhurst Club for the use of their courts on this and many other occasions.

My thanks are also due to Barbara Godfrey and Liza Huddlestone who did all the typing work.

CLAIRE CHAPMAN

Introduction

Squash is a game which is gaining rapidly in popularity as an optional activity in the fourth, fifth and sixth years at school. It is a relatively easy game to learn and fun to play at any level of ability. The equipment needed is not expensive and the only problem may be to find courts to play on. Although many Public schools have their own courts, most Local Authority schools will hire municipal or club courts each week for a small group of children to play. Some teachers taking these groups will be experienced players, but many will have played little or no squash and these notes have been put together with the needs of this whole range of ability in mind. They also cover the required syllabus for the L.E.A. coaching courses run by the two governing bodies of squash (included in the Appendix), the Squash Rackets Association and the Women's Squash Rackets Association.

The first part is an elementary introduction to the game, followed by a section on the technique of the various shots, their teaching points, and practices ranging from beginner to advanced level.

In an effort to clarify some of the problems that inexperienced players have in understanding the rules, a section is included to cover the rules, scoring, marking and refereeing.

Following this, there is a series of lesson plans and suggestions for further work.

For those who can spend enough time on the game to reach a higher level of play, there is a discussion on tactics beyond those of the elementary level, and some background information on the history and development of the game.

THE COURT

Front Wall

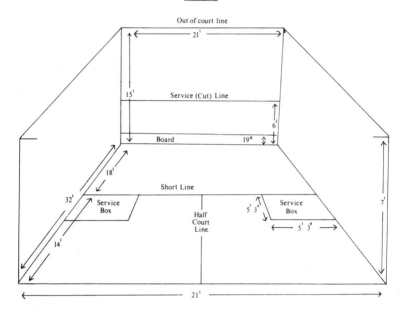

Fig. 1. Looking at the court through a glass back wall

The Game

Squash is played in a four-sided court with dimensions and markings that are shown in Figure 1.

Two players hit the ball alternately (a rally) on to the front wall, but it may touch any of the other walls before or after the front wall, except for the first shot in the rally (the service) which has to touch the front wall first.

The rally is ended when the ball touches the floor for the second time before a player hits it, fails to touch the front wall between the out of court line and the board, or touches anything on or above the out of court line.

Which player is to serve first is decided by one player spinning a racket and the other choosing which side will fall uppermost. The player winning the right to serve (Hand-in), stands in one of the service boxes and hits the ball directly on to the front wall above the service line, so that it lands in the opposite back quarter of the court.

Scoring goes with service, so that if Hand-in wins the rally, he scores a point, but if he loses it, neither player scores but the other player serves. The game normally ends when one player has scored nine points, but if they should reach a score of 8–8, then the non-server (Hand-out) who reached eight points first has the choice of playing up to nine points or up to ten to finish the game.

Should the service fail to touch the front wall above the service line, or to reach the opposite back quarter of the court, the server can have a second attempt, unless Hand-out chooses to hit it anyway. If he does, then the rally continues as usual. The service may of course be hit before it reaches the floor (volley). Each time Hand-in wins a rally and scores a point, he must then go and serve from the other service box.

If a player is unable to hit the ball because the other player is in the way and in danger of being hit by the racket or the ball, there is a 'let' and the rally is played again.

The aim is to hit the ball as far away from your opponent as possible, so that he cannot reach it before it bounces twice. Having hit the ball it is essential to get to the centre of the court (roughly where the short line and the half court line meet, the 'T') as quickly as possible, to be ready for the next shot. It is equally important to watch the ball and your opponent playing it so that you have some idea where his shot is going to go. This is more difficult in squash than most racket games, because some of the time your opponent is behind you on the court.

Technique

Considered in this section are the uses, teaching points and practices for the strokes. Some practices are for groups, others for an individual or pairs and they start with the relatively easy and progress on to the more difficult.

The descriptions and photographs of the grip and the strokes have been based on a right-handed player, so left-handed players will have to either reverse them or read Jonah Barrington's book listed in the Bibliography.

Certain fundamental points of technique have to be considered in relation to all the shots and they provide a convenient check list when trying to spot faults in a stroke.

STROKE FUNDAMENTALS

1. Grip—fortunately it is the same for all the strokes.
2. Position of the body in relation to the ball.
3. Footwork.
4. Swing of the racket—safety.
5. Control of the racket face.
6. Balance and transfer of weight.

There are other fundamentals of the game, rather than of a particular shot, which need to be considered, such as general positioning in the game, watching the ball, having the racket ready and movement round the court.

POSITION ON THE COURT

One of the basic tactical aims of the game is to try to return as quickly as possible after each shot to the middle of the court. This is usually taken to be the 'T' formed by the junction of the short and half court lines. In fact it is more sensible to stand a foot or two behind this and slightly towards the position of your opponent.

Having got there, the position to adopt is a slight crouch with the knees a little bent so that you can move off quickly. Between shots, you should hold your racket with the head higher than your hand, so that you can start the stroke quickly. The correct positioning and timing of the stroke is only possible if you are watching the ball, so that you can judge the point at which you should hit it.

In order to get some idea where you will have to move, it is essential to watch the ball and your opponent playing it, so that you can anticipate the next shot.

MOVEMENT ON THE COURT

To cover the ground quickly and easily, the modern squash player moves with a fairly long stride, trying to keep the ball in view, from the centre 'T' to a corner and back to the 'T'. This often involves a sort of sideways or backwards *chassé* rather than a run. It is important to keep well clear of the walls, so that your shot is not cramped, and to be well balanced as you play the stroke so that you can move quickly back into position again.

THE GRIP

There is little time in squash to change the grip, so it is essential to use a 'Continental' grip which does not need to be changed for the different strokes.

To assume the correct grip, hold the racket in the left hand with the racket at right angles to the ground. Then with the right hand, shake hands with the handle and curl the fingers round it, as shown in Figure 3, with the thumb across the back of the handle. This should result in a pronounced 'V' between the thumb and first finger, with the point of the 'V' slightly round to the left of the handle.

The first finger is placed rather like a 'trigger' finger on a pistol.

Top-class players do change their grip occasionally, perhaps

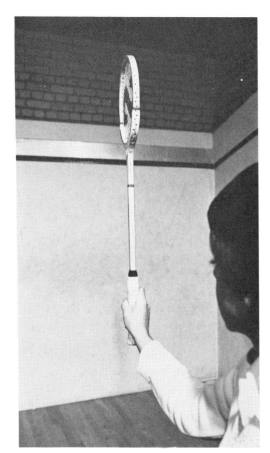

Fig. 2

Fig. 3

shifting nearer the racket head to get more control or to be able to pick up a shot from close to the back wall, and shifting more to the end of the handle to reach a shot at full stretch. They may also, given time, shift the grip slightly further round to the left, to get more power for a backhand shot, but complete control with the standard grip must be acquired first before considering any variations. The grip shown in the photographs is rather far up the handle and a more orthodox grip would show the butt of the handle resting on the heel of the hand.

BASIC LENGTH SHOTS

1. *The straight length shots* played after the ball has bounced on the floor are the most essential ones in the game: to move your opponent safely into the back corners, or to win the rally when your opponent is out of position. The good length shot is one which bounces for the second time close to the back wall. Where it bounces for the first time will depend on the height and power of the shot, as well as the speed of the ball. It helps if the ball touches the side wall behind the service box, as this will slow it down. If your shot is dropping short, you need to aim it higher on the front wall to increase the length.

The perfect length of course is the shot which catches the 'nick' (the join between the back wall and the floor). Depending on the situation, the ball may be hit early (soon after it bounces on the floor) to give your opponent less time, or late (after the top of the bounce) to give you more time to play an accurate shot when your opponent is in a good position. Also when you hit the ball late, your opponent may start to move, and you can then change your shot. Trying to hit the ball at its highest point on top of the bounce is usually reserved for the hard hit short kill, aimed into the side wall/floor 'nick', other hard cut shots and some drop shots.

The technique for the straight forehand and backhand length shots is pictured and described in some detail and only the differences from this are noted for the other strokes. In the early stages of learning the game, only a few points would be used and the others brought in to improve the stroke when your players can hit the ball fairly easily. Probably the most important points to emphasise at the beginning are:

1. Early backswing.
2. Sideways stance.
3. Watch ball.
4. Hit at comfortable distance opposite leading knee.

2. *Cross court length shots* have to be played with some care as they can be easily cut off by your opponent if he is in a good position in the middle of the court. To avoid this, play the shot when he is more on your side of the court and make sure that it is played very wide, to touch the side wall around the back of the service box.

Figs. 4, 5, and 6. Forehand drive

FOREHAND DRIVE

1. POSITION RELATIVE TO THE BALL

(*a*) Sideways stance. Note that the shoulders are turned towards the back corner.

(*b*) Watching the ball which is hit after it has bounced on the floor.

(*c*) Hit at a comfortable distance opposite the left knee.

2. FOOTWORK

(*a*) Stepping in with the left leg.

(*b*) Knee bent to get down to the ball.

3. THE SWING

(*a*) Early backswing with the elbow well bent to take the racket head high.

(*b*) Note the cocked wrist to get more power into the shot.

(*c*) Arm straight when the ball is hit.

(*d*) Bent elbow on the follow through to take the racket head high.

4. CONTROL OF RACKET FACE

(*a*) Racket face at right angles to the floor or slightly sloped back (open) at contact point.

5. BALANCE AND TRANSFER OF WEIGHT

(*a*) Wide stance for balance.

(*b*) The weight transferring from the right to the left foot through the stroke.

CROSS COURT FOREHAND

The only difference for the cross court shot is in the contact point, which is further forward, i.e. nearer to the front wall.

Fig. 7

Fig. 8

Fig. 9

BACKHAND DRIVE

1. POSITION RELATIVE TO THE BALL

   (*a*) Sideways stance. Note that the shoulders are in fact facing the back corner and the back of the right shoulder is towards the front wall.

   (*b*) Watching the ball which is hit after it has bounced on the floor.

   (*c*) Hit the ball at a comfortable distance opposite the right knee.

2. FOOTWORK

   (*a*) Stepping in with the right leg.

   (*b*) Right knee bent to get down to the ball.

3. THE SWING

   (*a*) Early backswing with a bent elbow to take the racket back high.

   (*b*) Bent elbow on the follow through to take the racket head high.

4. CONTROL OF THE RACKET FACE

(a) Racket face slightly open, i.e. sloping back on impact.

5. BALANCE AND TRANSFER OF WEIGHT

(a) Wide stance for balance.
(b) The weight transferring from the left to the right foot through the stroke.

CROSS COURT BACKHAND

Again as for the cross court forehand, the ball is hit when it is slightly further forward.

PRACTICES FOR STRAIGHT LENGTH SHOTS

Group
1. Team rally. The players are numbered 1–4 and move forward to hit the ball in turn (trying to keep it on the forehand or backhand side), then move out of the way. You need to watch the safety of this one and may have to hit the shot in between each of your players to keep the rally going at beginner level.
2. Circling exercises. With a group of players lined up as for feeding a forehand. Each one hits a straight shot in turn and then moves round to join the end of the line again.

Individual
1. Counting shots in a rally on the forehand or backhand.
2. As above, counting only the shots which land behind the short line.
3. Straight drive, aiming to get the ball to bounce in the service box, counting the number of consecutive shots which land in the target area.
4. Play alternate shots above and below the 'cut' line.
5. Play each shot to land inside a line chalked parallel to the side wall. Where you chalk the line depends on how severe you want the practice to be.

Pairs

1. One player hits an easy ball into mid court, while the other tries to hit it to a perfect length.
2. Have a rally with your partner in one half (side) of the court. This can be made more difficult by using a chalked corridor.
3. Player 'A' plays an angle from behind the short line, while player 'B' returns it with a straight length shot. Player 'A' returns this with an angle from the other side of the court and player 'B' returns it with a straight length shot.
4. With one player standing around the short line to cut the ball off on the volley, the other tries to get the ball past him along the side wall.

PRACTICE GAMES

1. One player has to try to return every shot to a length, while the other plays his normal game. You can also play this game so that the length player is only allowed to make winners at the back of the court.
2. One player has to return every shot down the nearest side wall.

PRACTICES FOR CROSS COURT LENGTH SHOTS

1. Put an easy ball up in mid-court, or have a partner do this, then try to hit it to touch the side wall near the floor, just behind the service box.
2. Have a rally with a partner, each player trying to hit the side wall near the back of the service box.
3. Three-shot sequence with a partner, consisting of: player 'A', boast; player 'B', cross court drive; player 'A', straight drive; player 'B', boast, etc.

THE SERVE

There are many types of serve, but the two most commonly used are the high lob and the low hard length. The path of the ball and the position of the players for the serve is shown in Figures 10 and 11. Which one you use depends on how well you play them, which one your opponent does not like, the court, and the state of the game. The aim for either of these serves is to put your opponent on the defensive, so that he cannot attack the serve except by playing a very risky shot, and occasionally you may even win a point outright. The serve must be accurate or your opponent may be able to play a winner from it, or get you out of position.

1. HIGH LOB SERVE

The position you play the shot in is not as important as where it goes, but it should at least be consistent, so that you can develop an accurate serve. Since you have to move to the middle of the court immediately after the serve, it is usual to stand as near to the centre 'T' as possible, and one foot must be on the ground inside the lines of the service box. The ball should hit the front wall near the 'out of court' line and go up even higher, before dropping down to touch the side wall high up, level with the back of the service box. It should then drop to the floor at the back of the court to a length. There are many ways of playing this stroke, but the easiest one for beginners is to start with the racket low and the left shoulder pointing to the spot on the front wall where the ball is aimed. The ball is thrown up a short distance or allowed to drop, and the racket brought up to hit the underside of the ball. This serve takes little effort and well played is difficult to return effectively.

2. HARD LENGTH SERVE

The position is the same as for the lob serve and the ball can be hit slightly above shoulder level or as an overarm shot similar to a tennis serve. It is usually played to hit the front wall just above the 'cut' line, touching the side wall low down near the back of the service box, going to a length at the back of the court.

A useful variation particularly after a long, exhausting rally, is to serve straight at the player or down the middle of the court.

Figs. 10 and 11. Path of the ball in the two most common serves, with the position of the Server (Hand-in) and Receiver (Hand-out)

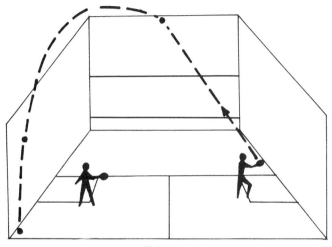

High lob serve

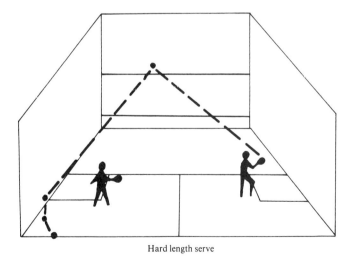

Hard length serve

PRACTICES FOR THE SERVE

1. Target practice, trying to get the serve to drop into a marked square in the back corners of the court.
2. In pairs, with each player having ten serves. The server scores one point if the receiver fails to make a good return. The receiver scores a point if he can make a winning return or if the serve is out of court. Neither player scores if the serve is returned and the server can reply with a good return.

RETURN OF SERVICE

The aim in returning serve is to move your opponent from his position in the middle of the court and into a corner. The safest way to do this is with a high straight shot close to the side wall. This should be your standard return and unless the serve has been played very short, your shot will have to be a volley.

The usual position is for the receiver to stand about a foot behind the outside back corner of the service box, turned slightly towards the side wall, but watching the server, in case he hits an unexpected one down the middle or straight at you. The racket head should be kept well up, as you will probably have to volley the serve. Should your opponent move too far across, perhaps expecting your usual

Figs. 12, 13 and 14. Possible service returns

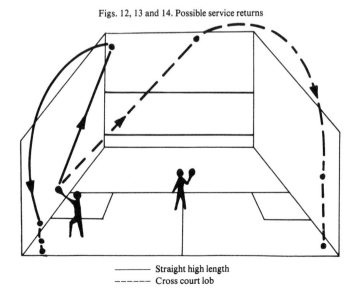

———— Straight high length
– – – – Cross court lob

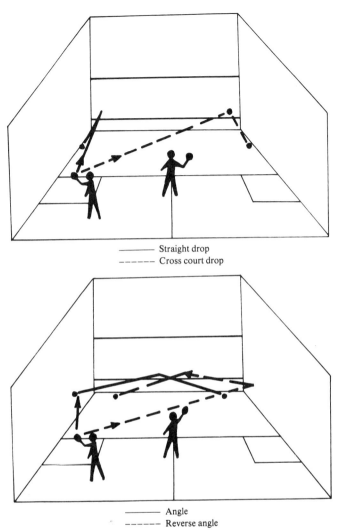

——— Straight drop
- - - - - Cross court drop

——— Angle
- - - - - Reverse angle

straight return, then an equally good return is to volley the ball high up onto the front wall to drop in the opposite back corner. If the serve is a poor one, then you might attack it if you are sure of your shot. Possible alternative returns, then, might be a drop or cross court drop, an angle or reverse angle, and these might be played either on the volley or after the ball has bounced. All these service returns are shown in Figures 12, 13 and 14.

THE VOLLEY

The volley (hitting the ball before it touches the ground) has already been mentioned as the best return of a good serve and it is also the best way to put pressure on your opponent, giving him far less time to get to the shot. It is pointless to volley unless it is a good one, as you may be left stranded by a fast reply from your opponent. The volley may be played as a straight or cross court length shot or cut short into the front corner either straight, across the court, or angled.

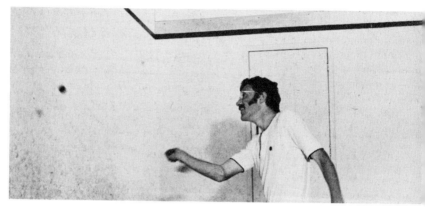

Fig. 15

Fig. 16. (*below*) Forehand length volley

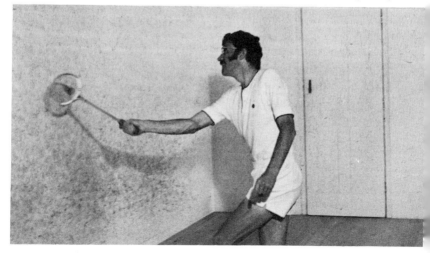

Fig. 17. Backhand length volley

1. LENGTH VOLLEY

If there is time, you should use the same sideways stance as for the forehand and backhand drives, and hit the ball opposite the leading shoulder, well away from the body. The stroke is played with a shorter backswing and a 'punch' action, with the wrist held firm. The racket face is slightly open and the ball aimed to hit the front wall above the 'cut' line. The follow through takes the racket towards the spot the ball is aimed to hit on the front wall. These points are shown in the photographs of the forehand and backhand volley.

2. THE SHORT VOLLEY

This has to be hit when it is in front of the leading shoulder, to bring it down to the front wall just above the tin, aiming to hit the side wall/floor 'nick' a short distance from the front wall. At a more advanced level, slight side slice can be used to help bring the short cross court volley into the side wall and take some pace off the ball.

You need to be sure that your opponent is behind you when you play the short volley.

PRACTICES FOR THE VOLLEY

1. Set up a high shot in the middle of the court or get a partner to do this and try to volley to a length.
2. Play a volley rally with yourself, counting consecutive shots played from behind the 'short' line. The position should be varied, so that you try a rally from behind the service box and also from well in front of the 'short' line.
3. One player serves and the other volleys to a length.
4. Set up a high shot or get a partner to do this and volley short, aiming for the 'nick'.
5. With the same set up, play 3 length volleys and then a short one, straight or across court.
6. Play a volley rally across the court to a partner, from behind the 'short' line. Make a game out of this by scoring a point each time your shot hits the floor on your partner's side.
7. One player stands around the 'short' line trying to cut the ball off on the volley, while the other player at the back of the court tries to get the ball past him along the side wall.
8. One player hits high cross court shots from the back of the court, which the other player tries to cut off with a straight volley played either to a length or short.
9. Player 'A' boasts, player 'B' hits a cross court lob, player 'A' hits a straight length volley, player 'B' boasts, etc.

THE ANGLE OR SIDE WALL SHOT

A shot which hits the side wall before the front wall may be called an angle, a side wall shot or boast. However, the term 'boast' is here reserved for the shot played from the back corners and any shot played on to the side wall from further up the court is called an angle. A perfect angle bounces into the side wall/floor 'nick' but a very good one hits the front wall just above the tin and takes its second bounce on the floor before reaching the other side wall. The most

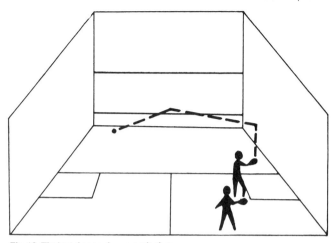

Fig. 18. The best time to play an angle shot

Fig. 19. Backhand angle

Figs. 20 and 21. Forehand angle

effective angle is played when your opponent is behind you on your side of the court. This situation is shown in Figure 18. Although the angle should not usually be played when your opponent is in front of you, it can also be most effectively played when he is coming back quickly from the diagonally opposite front corner, expecting a straight length shot. The angle is also valuable as a way of returning a ball which has gone too far past you for a straight shot to be possible. The shot can also be played as a volley.

TEACHING POINTS

1. The angle is usually played using the same position relative to the ball as for the straight drive, but merely turning further round. This is shown in the photograph of the backhand angle (Figure 19).
2. As a development, a more deceptive method is to take up the same position as in the straight drive, but hit the ball rather later (opposite the middle of the body).
3. Also different is the racket face, which is rather more 'open'. This gives the necessary lift for the ball to reach the front wall and it also imparts some 'cut' to the ball, so that it comes more quickly off the front wall and dies rapidly when it hits the floor. These points can be seen in the photographs of the forehand angle.

PRACTICES FOR ANGLE SHOTS

1. Throw the ball on to the side wall (behind the short line) and play an angle.
2. One player feeds the ball from the front of the court on to the side wall, for the other to play an angle.
3. Using the same set up, try to make the angle bounce on the floor in front of a line chalked a few feet from and parallel to the front wall.
4. Player 'A' plays a straight length shot, which player 'B' returns with an angle. Player 'A' returns this with a straight length shot along the other side wall and player 'B' returns this with an angle. This can equally well be used with three players, so that player 'A'

returns both the angles with straight length shots as before, with player 'B' playing the forehand angle and player 'C' the backhand angle. If you are really short of courts and your players are both well controlled and fast about the court, then you can even try it with four players.

5. The straight shot is played high, so that the angle has to be taken on the volley.

6. Three or four straight length volleys, then angle.

GAMES FOR ANGLE SHOTS

1. You can play an angle only game, using the area of court in front of the short line. The game is started by one player hitting a gentle shot on to the front wall, but from then on every shot must be an angle, so the ball must hit the side wall first. The winner of the rally scores a point, regardless of who had the service, and the game goes up to nine points. The service is taken by each player in turn.

THE LOB

This is a slow high shot, used to give you time to get back into position after stretching to reach a ball at the front of the court, and also if your opponent has come rather too far forward in the court.

It can be played straight, but is usually across the court where there is less danger of the ball going out of court, and has a similar path to the lob serve.

The ball goes very high at the front of the court, dropping down to the floor at the back of the court.

To get the necessary height, the ball is usually hit well in front of you and stroked up on to the front wall. To hit the ball in this position, the general stance is rather more towards the front wall, with the shoulders facing the front corner, and the knees well bent so that you can get your racket under the ball.

Although usually played from a ball that has bounced, it can also be hit on the volley, again with the object of gaining time to get back into a good position.

PRACTICES FOR THE LOB

1. Set a ball up in the front of the court, or get a partner to do this, and then lob across the court. It is useful to have a third player who stands on the 'T' to volley any lobs which are within his range. This helps to make the lobber realise how much height and width he has to get on the shot.
2. Using the same set up, play the straight lob.
3. One player lobs across court and the other returns it with a boast from the back of the court. A third player can help here as in the first practice.

THE DROP SHOT

The best time to play a drop shot is when you are at or just in front of the 'short' line and your opponent is behind you. Played from further back, there is a larger element of risk involved. If you are close to the front corner, your opponent, if he has not had to stretch to reach the last shot, is likely to be on your heels, unless your intentions are well disguised.

The shot is aimed to hit the front wall just above the tin and drop short into the side wall/floor 'nick'. The backswing and sideways stance should be the same as for the normal drive and the racket face slightly open, to cut the ball, taking some of the pace off it. The contact point is slightly ahead of the leading foot and the ball guided, pushed or stroked on to the front wall, with a short follow through, the racket ending up pointing to the spot on the front wall where the ball was aimed. No power is needed for the shot, so there is no transference of weight through the shot, the weight being on the leading foot before the ball is hit, to provide perfect balance. The photographs of a backhand drop shot (Figures 22–24) show these points quite clearly. The drop shot can also be played across the court as a variation from the straight drop shot.

PRACTICES FOR THE DROP SHOT

1. Either set the ball up in mid court or get a partner to do it and play a drop shot from this.

2. One player hits an angle or boast from the back of the court and the other tries to play a drop shot that they cannot return.

3. One player hits an angle or boast from the back of the court and the other plays the drop shot. The first player returns another drop and the players alternate hitting drop shots until they fail to make a good return.

4. Player 'A' boasts, player 'B' plays a drop shot, player 'A' plays a straight lob, player 'B' plays the boast, etc.

5. Play a game in which one player has to make all his winners with shots to the front of the court. This brings in not only drop shots, but all the other short shots as well.

Figs. 22–24. Backhand drop sho

Fig. 23

Fig. 24

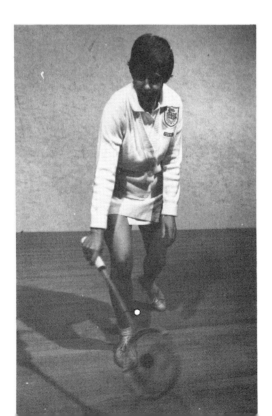

Fig. 25

THE BOAST

This is a deep angle shot to retrieve a ball in the back corner. There is not enough room for the normal positioning without hitting the back wall on the back swing so this has to be changed. To make room for a full swing, you need to turn further round and face the back wall. The racket face is open to give the ball enough lift to reach the front wall and the ball is hit well out to the side of the body, between the side wall and the foot nearest to it. These points are shown clearly in the photographs of the backhand boast (Figures 25–27). The shot can, and sometimes has, to be played on the volley, if the ball would otherwise drop to a perfect length at the back of the court. The ball is hit fairly high on to the side wall, to finish up in the opposite front corner.

PRACTICES FOR THE BOAST

1. Throw the ball on to the side wall near the back of the court and play a boast to the front corner. This can be made more difficult

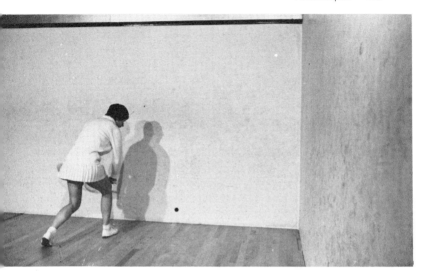

Fig. 26

Fig. 27

by throwing the ball so that it goes side wall–back wall, dropping down close to the back wall.

2. One player hits a cross court lob and the other returns this with the boast.
3. Player 'A' boasts, player 'B' hits cross court shot, player 'A' hits straight shot, player 'B' boasts, etc.

BOASTED LOB OR SKID BOAST

This is a variation on the standard boast, played harder, further forward, and much higher on to the side wall, so that it hits the front wall very high and screws back across the middle of the court into the opposite back corner. It is a difficult shot to play but can be very effective when your opponent is expecting the standard shot and has started drifting towards the front corner. Curiously enough this shot was used quite often in the late 1920s, according to Charles Reed (1929), when the faster ball made this the obvious way of playing a cross court lob. Roshan Khan seems to have reintroduced it to a present-day group of players from Pakistan and they use it very effectively.

REVERSE ANGLE

This is an angle shot played on to the side wall furthest away from you, so that it ends up in the front corner on your own side of the court.

It is most effectively played when your opponent is behind you and on the other side of the court. As the shot goes across in front of your opponent, he cannot start to move until it has been played. The reverse angle can be played on the volley as well or after the ball has bounced and if it is accurate, can be a devastating return of a rather short serve or any poor length shot. The actual path of the ball is shown in Figure 27, illustrating service returns.

PRACTICES FOR THE REVERSE ANGLE

1. One player sets the ball up in mid court and the other plays a reverse angle.

2. The angle only game played in front of the short line, scoring a point for each rally won, up to nine points and started by one player hitting a gentle shot on to the front wall.

CRASH KILL INTO THE 'NICK'

This shot seems to have been introduced into the game by Hashim Khan, who seemed to have an unerring aim for the side wall/floor 'nick', either straight or across the court, a few feet from the front wall.

To get enough power and the right line for the shot, it has to be hit either at the top of the bounce or as a shoulder height volley. Some players hit the ball with the racket face flat or even closed, and others use a certain amount of 'cut', whipping the racket face down the back of the ball as it is hit. This makes for better control, but does reduce the power of the shot.

The only way to find out which suits you best is to experiment with both methods.

PRACTICES FOR THE CRASH KILL

1. Either set the ball up for yourself, or get a partner to do this, so that you can practise the shot as a ground stroke and as a volley.

Spotting and Correcting Faults

In order to help your players to improve a poor stroke, it is essential to be able to spot the fault or faults that are causing this. It may not be a fault of stroke technique, but a fault in general positioning or tactics, so that the player gets to the ball too late to play a reasonable shot, or tries to play the wrong shot. To see where the stroke itself is going wrong, you need to run through the fundamental points for all strokes and then check the teaching points for the stroke.

1. WATCHING THE BALL

Missing the ball or mis-timing the shot, may be caused by failure to watch the ball. Not watching your opponent hit the ball makes anticipation difficult, so that the player is slow in moving to the ball.

2. THE GRIP

Is it really a 'Continental'?, with the point of the 'V' (formed by thumb and forefinger) slightly round to the left of the handle when the racket head is vertical to the ground.

A heavy slice on the backhand may be caused by a 'Western' forehand grip, where the point of the 'V' is well round to the right of the handle.

3. POSITION OF THE BODY IN RELATION TO THE BALL

Correct positioning for the straight drive should show the shoulders facing the side wall for an easy-paced forehand shot. More turn towards the back corners is needed for the backhand and to generate greater pace on the forehand.

For the cross court shot, the shoulders face the side wall, slightly towards the front corner, while for the angle, the shoulders face the back corner.

Failure to turn enough causes a straight shot to go across court, a cross court to go too wide (also resulting in a dangerous follow through) and an angle to hit the side wall too far forward.

If the shoulder position is correct, then the most frequent error when trying to play a straight shot is to hit the ball when it is too far ahead, i.e. nearer the front wall than the leading foot. This causes the ball to go across the court behind the striker, or to go too high. The ball hit when it is too far back hits the side wall before the front wall.

Remember that changing the contact point but keeping the body position constant is a more advanced way of playing the three alternatives i.e. straight drive, cross court and angle.

4. FOOTWORK

Incorrect footwork makes it difficult to get an adequate turn and backswing, particularly on the backhand side.

This results in a rather weak stroke and a tendency to pull the ball across court.

It is essential to get into the habit as soon as possible of stepping in on the left foot for the forehand and the right foot for the backhand.

5. SWING

The most common fault associated with the swing is to start too late. The backswing should start as soon as the opponent's shot hits the front wall.

The swing itself should be whatever is appropriate to the shot, i.e. a 'throwing' action for the drives and angles, more of a 'punch' for the volley and something closer to a push for the drop shot.

A pendulum type of swing causes the shot to go too high and a cramped swing with the ball taken too close to the body is a frequent cause of missed or mis-hit strokes.

To allow a free stroke and also to save on the distance that has to be covered, the ball should be hit at a comfortable distance from the body, with the racket almost parallel to the ground.

At a more advanced level, to generate greater pace in the shot, the wrist is 'cocked' (extension with radial deviation) on the backswing, so that the racket head lags well behind the hand and can be whipped through fast as the ball is hit.

Flexing the wrist on the backswing is a fairly common fault in the backhand drive, leading to poor control and a weak shot. This is difficult to correct, but it does help if the player tries to keep the wrist 'cocked' through the stroke.

6. CONTROL OF RACKET FACE

Most shots in squash are played with the racket face slightly 'open', i.e. with the top edge sloped back. This is more marked for backhands and also for angles, boasts and lobs, because the 'open' face gives the extra lift for these shots.

Hard hit forehands, particularly those aimed to the 'nick', are more often played 'flat' or with the racket face slightly 'closed', i.e. with the top edge sloped slightly forward. An excessively 'open' or 'closed' racket face is usually the result of an incorrect grip.

7. BALANCE AND TRANSFER OF WEIGHT

Is the player well enough balanced to play the shot? Failure to get to the right place in time to be well balanced for the shot is likely to cause mis-timing and makes it difficult for the player to move back in to position quickly.

The weight should transfer from the back to the front foot as the stroke is played and failure to do this tends to cause a high, weak shot and difficulty in playing a straight shot.

An exception to this is the drop shot which should be played with the weight on the leading foot throughout the stroke. No power is needed for this shot and it is likely to be more accurate if the player is steady and well balanced.

If the weight has transferred correctly on to the front foot, it should be possible to lift the back foot off the ground without falling over.

8. OTHER SOURCES OF ERROR

The cause of a poor stroke may well be failure to understand where the ball should be aimed on the side or front wall to achieve the desired result. This happens most often with angles or cross court shots, because players do not always realise how the ball will rebound off the wall.

An angle shot which fails to reach the front wall may simply be too weak or too low, but more often has not been played to touch the side wall far enough forward for the rebound to carry to the front wall.

Another similar error is the service or cross court shot which constantly goes out of court on the side wall or comes into the middle of the court because it has been aimed too far past the middle of the front wall and therefore rebounded on to the side wall too near the front wall.

CORRECTION OF FAULTS

Spotting a fault is difficult enough, but it is often hard to decide which particular fault is the most important one to correct in trying to improve a stroke. Only experience can help you with this one, although the order in which the fundamental points are covered gives you something to go on. The sequence is the same as the basic teaching of a stroke:

1. Explanation/Demonstration.
2. Feed a simple shot from which your pupil can play the stroke.
3. Set up a shot sequence to include the stroke.
4. Use the stroke in a game, setting up situations where it can be played.

It is important not to over correct, particularly in the early stages of learning the game, or the interest and enjoyment of your pupils may be destroyed.

Sooner or later you will come across a player who is totally incapable of hitting the ball and the following suggestions, starting with the very simple and progressing to the fairly simple, may help you to start them off:

1. Stand your player close to a wall with the ball balanced on the racket face. Get them to push it on to the wall and try to hit it back again after it has bounced on the floor.
2. Throw or hit the ball on to the wall so that they can hit it back on to the wall after the bounce without having to move.
3. Get them to throw the ball on to the wall and then hit it after it has bounced.
4. With the racket held low, they can drop the ball and bring the racket up to meet it, to hit the ball on to the wall.
5. Gradually move your player further back in the court as they succeed with these simple practices until they can drop and hit the ball to reach the front wall and return a simple shot which you have played on to the front wall.

The Rules, Marking and Refereeing

The important rules governing play are grouped into those concerning service, being hit by the ball, obstruction, match play, and the calls and duties of the marker and referee.

SERVICE RULES

1. The server is known as 'Hand-in' and must stand with at least one foot on the floor, within the lines of the service box. At the start of a game, or when he wins the service, he may serve from either box, but if he wins the rally, must then serve from the opposite side. He continues to serve from alternate service boxes until he loses a rally and his opponent wins the service.
2. The server throws the ball up and hits it on to the front wall between the 'cut' line and the 'out of court' line.
3. The ball must drop on to the floor within the lines marking the opposite back quarter of the court, unless 'Hand-out' chooses to hit the ball before it touches the floor.

FAULTS

The service is a fault and the server can have a second serve in the following circumstances.
1. One foot is not on the floor within the lines of the service box.
2. The ball hits the front wall on or below the 'cut' line.
3. The ball fails to reach the opposite back quarter of the court. 'Hand-out' may, if he chooses, play the fault serve and the rally continues, as this annuls the fault.

SERVING YOUR HAND OUT

The server loses the service or 'serves his hand out' in the following ways.

1. Serving two single faults in succession.
2. If the ball goes out of court, i.e. on or above the 'out of court' line, on to the 'board' or the 'tin'.
3. The ball hits any part of the court before the front wall.
4. If the server misses the ball, or hits it more than once.
5. If the ball comes back and touches the server, his racket or clothes before it has bounced twice.

APPEALS ON SERVICE

The server may appeal against a call of 'Fault', and 'Hand-out' may appeal that a fault was not called, but only under certain conditions.

THE SERVER ('Hand-in')

1. May *not* appeal against a call of 'Footfault'.
2. May *not* appeal against a call of 'Fault' to the first serve.
3. May appeal against a call of 'Fault' to the second serve. If allowed, a let is played and the second serve taken again.

THE RECEIVER ('Hand-out')

1. May only appeal that the *first* serve was a 'fault' or 'out of court' if he does not play a stroke at it. If his appeal were rejected, he would then of course lose the point.
2. May appeal that the *second* serve was a 'fault' or 'out of court' even if he plays the stroke and will usually do so at the end of the rally. If the referee or the marker acting as referee decides that it was a fault, then 'Hand-out' gains the service. Should there be a doubt, then a 'let' is allowed and the service played again.

If there has been a 'fault' called on the first service this is not annulled by the 'let'. The server retains the point if the referee is quite certain that the serve was good.

BEING HIT BY THE BALL

When a player is hit by the ball the decision depends on whether he was hit by his own shot or his opponent's, the direction the ball was taking and the positions of the players.

1. If your opponent hits you with a ball that was going straight to the front wall and would have made a good return, i.e., between the top and bottom 'out of court' lines, then he wins the rally.

   However, there are two exceptions to this rule:

(a) If your opponent has shaped to hit the ball in front of you, and is hitting it at the second attempt, then a 'let' is allowed and the rally replayed.

(b) If your opponent has followed the ball round the back corner of the court and 'turned' before making the stroke, a 'let' is again allowed.

2. If your opponent hits you with a ball which would have been a good return, but would have hit another wall first, then a 'let' is allowed.

3. If your opponent hits you with a ball which would not have been a good return, then he loses the rally.

4. If your own shot hits you, your racket or clothes, before it bounces twice, then you lose the rally. There is one exception to this, which is that if your opponent is in such a position that he is preventing you from getting out of the way, or has shaped to hit the ball in front of you, then a 'let' is allowed.

5. If your opponent tries to hit the ball in front of you but misses and is in no position to make a second attempt to hit it, then you win the rally even if the ball hits you.

OBSTRUCTION

A player must do his best to give his opponent a clear view of the ball, and enough room to play his stroke on to any part of the front wall, or the side wall near the front wall. Should a player fail to do this, then according to the circumstances, the striker may be awarded a 'let' or a 'penalty point'. Note that an excessive backswing or follow through which does not allow a player time or space to reach the ball, may be considered as 'Obstruction'.

1. When it's a 'Let'

(a) When a player has tried, but failed, to get out of the way, and the striker was not in an obvious winning position, then a 'let' is allowed, if the striker does not try to play the ball and asks the marker (referee, if there is one) for a 'let'.

(b) A 'let' will also be allowed on appeal to the marker if a player hits his opponent with his racket while playing the stroke and fails to make a good return.

2. When it's a Point

The marker will award the rally to the striker either on appeal (or in some cases without waiting for an appeal), in the following cases:

(a) When a player, in the opinion of the marker, has not done his best to get out of the way, or give his opponent a fair view of the ball.

(b) Even though a player has done his best to get out of the way, he has prevented the striker from playing an obvious winning stroke. This is likely to occur in two situations, firstly, when a player having just scraped up a shot at the front of the court, is too off balance to move out of the way, and his opponent cannot hit the ball without hitting him at the same time. The other situation occurs at the back of the court, when a player has played a shot which is coming back towards him, and fails to get back far enough for his opponent to have room to play his obvious winner to the front of the court.

(c) When a player, having tried to hit a straight shot parallel to the side wall, mis-hits the ball so that it comes back between himself and the centre of the court. In his eagerness to get back into position in the centre, he jumps across the flight of his own shot and in doing so prevents his opponent from either hitting the ball, or seeing it in time to hit it.

(d) When it is absolutely certain that a player would hit his oponent with a ball going straight to the front wall, but for fear of injuring his opponent, he does not play the stroke.

In all these cases, the player who is prevented from making the stroke will appeal to the marker for a 'let' and it is up to the referee to decide whether he is entitled to one (i.e. could he have reached the ball) or if, in fact, he should be awarded the rally. If the referee sees that a dangerous situation is developing which is bound to lead to a 'point', then he can stop the rally without waiting for an appeal by the player.

MATCH PLAY

When your players reach the stage of playing matches, there are some more rules they will need to be familiar with:

1. A match is normally the best of five games, and the players are allowed to knock-up for five minutes before the match starts. It is usual for them to hit the ball to each other, using the match ball, changing sides after $2\frac{1}{2}$ minutes. This is timed by the marker. However, they may each knock-up separately with the ball on the match court for five minutes, deciding who has the first hit by spinning a racket.
2. A one minute rest is allowed between games, and if the score reaches two games each, then two minutes rest is allowed before the start of the fifth game. Apart from this, play should be continuous and no player may leave the court without the permission of the referee. If a match is unfinished for any reason and resumed the next day, it will be started from the beginning unless both players choose to start from the previous score.
3. Apart from the five minutes knock-up time, the players may not practise on any court the match may be played on within an hour of the scheduled time of the match.
4. A player not present within ten minutes of the scheduled time of the match may be disqualified by the referee.
5. A match is normally controlled by a 'marker', assisted by a 'referee', but if a referee is not available, the marker will carry out the duties of both.

DUTIES OF THE MARKER

The marker has to call faults, foot faults, not up, out of court and also repeat the decisions of the referee. He also has to keep a note of the score and the side a player is serving from. To do this, he needs a system for writing down the score, and the following works quite well.

Player 'A' is serving first.

$$\begin{array}{c|ll} A & 0^r \\ \hline B & \end{array}$$

Note that the server is starting from the right hand court, as indicated by the 'r' above his score.

If player 'A' wins this rally and therefore wins a point, the score sheet will look like this

$$\begin{array}{c|ll} A & 0^r & 1 \\ \hline B & \end{array}$$

Should player 'B' win the next rally and take over the serve, it will be noted as follows

$$\begin{array}{c|ll|l} A & 0^r & 1 \\ \hline B & & & 0_r \end{array}$$

Note that the server's score is always put ahead of the receiver's. It is a good idea to put a line after the serve changes hands, to make this clearer.

Player 'A' wins the next three rallies, making the score sheet look as follows

$$\begin{array}{c|ll|l|lll} A & 0^r & 1 & & 1^l & 2^r & 3 \\ \hline B & & & 0_r & & & \end{array}$$

Note the 'l' after the one, indicating that he is taking the serve from the left hand court.

It is also a good idea to write F = fault or X = let above the score when these occur in the game. Also note the starting time and the time each game ends.

CALLS OF THE MARKER

The marker has a number of standard calls which he uses to control the game, and they are as follows:

1. Time

This is normally called by the referee when there is one, but when the marker is also acting as referee he uses this call on three different occasions.

(a) When the five minute knock-up period is completed, to tell the players that it is time for the match to start.

(b) At the end of the rest period between games, when it is time for the next game to start.

(c) If at any time he wishes to stop play. This may be because a player serves before 'Hand-out' or the marker is ready, or if he notices that something has dropped into the court which might distract or injure a player.

Also, when there is no referee and the marker is carrying out the duties of the referee, he can stop play if he sees that a dangerous situation is developing, where a penalty point will be inevitable. He may also stop play to warn a player that he is crowding too close to his opponent, or that his swing is excessive.

2. Love-all

The marker calls the starting score of 0–0 as 'Love-all', and this is the signal to the server to begin.

After 'Time' has been called at the end of the knock-up, the players spin a racket to decide who serves, and tell the marker, who will then announce the match as follows:

'Semi-final match in the Middlesex Open Tournament, between Tom Smith and Joe Bloggs, Joe Bloggs to serve, Tom Smith to receive, best of five games, Love-all.'

3. Footfault or Fault

The marker should call a footfault or a fault very quickly, because 'Hand out' may, if he wishes, play the fault serve, and a late call will put him off his stroke.

If the marker calls a fault and 'Hand out' decides not to play the ball, the marker calls it like this—'one fault, 4–3' or whatever the score happens to be, and the calling of the score is the signal for the server to hit his second serve. Should a 'let' be called in this rally, it does not annul the previous fault and the marker calls as follows—'let ball, one fault, 4–3'.

Note that the score of the server is always called first.

4. Hand Out

When the server loses a rally and serves his hand out, the marker calls 'Hand out, 3–4', to indicate that the other player is now to serve. Note that the score has been reversed, so that the score of the new server is called first.

5. 'Let' Ball

A 'let' is allowed by the marker when acting as referee and the rally re-played, when:

(a) If 'Hand out' is not ready and does not attempt to play the serve.
(b) A ball breaks during play.
(c) The ball hits something lying in the court.
(d) The marker also repeats the decision of the referee to the players, if he has allowed a 'let' for some reason, or will allow a 'let' himself if he has doubts about one of his own decisions. Unless the marker is quite sure that a ball is out of court or has bounced twice, he will allow play to continue, and expect that, if the aggrieved player loses it, he will appeal about the doubtful stroke at the end of the rally. The marker's call is 'Let ball, 3–4'.

6. Not Up

This is the call if the marker is sure that a ball has touched the ground for the second time before a player hits it, or hits the board on the front wall. He calls 'Not up, 4–all'. Or if it was the server who had not got the ball up, it would be 'Not up, "hand out", 4–3'.

7. Out of Court

A ball is called out of court if it hits on or above the upper red line on any of the walls. The marker calls in the same way as for a ball that is not up, i.e. 'Out of court, 4–all'. Or 'Out of court, "hand out", 4–3'.

8. Game Ball

When the score reaches a stage where the server will win the game if he wins the next rally, the marker adds the call of 'Game ball' to the score, i.e. '8–3, game ball'; or if the game has been 'set to two', it would be '9–8, game ball'.

9. Set Two or No Set

If the score reaches 8-all, the receiver (Hand-out) has to choose whether to 'Set Two', in which the game will finish when one player gets ten points, or 'No Set' when the game will finish at the usual nine points. The next rally may not start until this decision has been made, and the marker will announce it as follows—'Set two, 8-all', or if no set has been chosen, it would be '8-all, no set, game ball'. The marker has to repeat these calls each time they are appropriate to the situation.

10. Other Calls

The marker also has to repeat the decisions of the referee, or make them himself if there is no referee, to award a 'let' or a 'point' to a player, or 'no let', in cases of obstruction or appeals against his decisions. He calls them as follows—'Let ball, 4–3', or 'Point to Smith, hand out, 3–4', or 'No let, 4–all'.

DUTIES OF THE REFEREE

The function of the referee is to ensure that each rally and every game reaches a fair conclusion. All appeals for obstruction, or against the decisions of the marker are made to the referee, who gives the players his decision. The players may not appeal against the decisions of the referee, or the marker when he is acting as the referee. He has various other functions as follows:

1. To keep a check on the score, so that on appeal from one of the players, he will know whether the marker's calling of the score is correct. He should without an appeal correct the marker's scoring or calling if he is certain that it is wrong.
2. To check that play is started after the five minute knock-up, and after the correct intervals between games.
3. A player may not leave the court without his permission, and he may order a player who has left the court to play on.
4. He may award a match to a player if his opponent has not turned up within ten minutes of the scheduled time.
5. He may stop play to warn a player that he is crowding or obstructing his opponent in some way, or not giving him a fair view of the ball, or that he is time-wasting, or distracting his opponent.
6. In extreme cases of misbehaviour he may order a player to leave the court and award the match to his opponent.
7. He should make sure that the spectators keep quiet and do not distract the players.
8. He should keep a spare ball in his pocket, in case the one in use breaks.
9. He should ensure that both players are wearing the correct all-white clothing, and that their shoes do not have black soles.

Note that if no referee is appointed for a match, all these duties are taken over by the marker, including making decisions on appeals against his own calls. When one person is fulfilling both duties, he has to make his decisions and call quickly. If he is doubtful about a particular shot, he will allow play to continue, and at the end of the rally when the player appeals, for instance, that his opponent's shot went out of court, then he can decide, having had time for reflection, either that the shot was good or that his original decision was wrong and the shot was out of court. In this second case he will award the rally to the appealing player, but if he remains in doubt will ask for a 'let' to be played.

Lesson Plans for Group Teaching

GENERAL POINTS

Unless you are fortunate enough to have a lot of time and a great many courts available for squash, you will be giving instruction mostly on a group basis, but the same principles and practices can be used in individual coaching.

Four players to a court is quite enough, if you are to ensure their safety and avoid too much waiting around.

Be sure that the whole group can see your demonstrations and organise the session so that they are kept active, are learning about the game and are enjoying it.

Squash is a relatively easy game and with a bit of help and encouragement, and the chance to hit the ball often enough, your group should be able to play some sort of a game by the end of the first lesson.

Normal P.E. kit should be worn and games shoes (not with black soles, as these mark the courts).

Ideally they should each have a racket and a ball (fast).

SQUASH BALLS

There are now four speeds of ball standardised by the SRA and distinguished by a different coloured spot.

Yellow spot—Slow ball used for match play or very hot courts.

White spot—Slightly faster for play or matches on cold courts. A good choice for most coaching.

Red spot—Faster ball for very cold courts or for coaching beginners.

Blue spot—Even faster ball for coaching young beginners on very cold courts.

The balls most often used for coaching are the white or red spot, and which one you use depends on the temperature of your courts. As black-surfaced balls make dark marks on the court walls, many clubs insist on the use of a green-surfaced ball, which is made in the same four speeds, with the same spot markings.

RACKETS

To play an orthodox squash stroke, it is essential to be able to whip the head of the racket through very fast and therefore the racket needs to be light and well balanced. The actual weight of the racket used will depend on the strength of your players, but it is interesting to note that Ken Hiscoe, who must be one of the sturdiest and strongest squash players, uses a racket which is lighter than that currently used by many women.

Janet Morgan and Heather McKay, who between them have dominated the women's game for the last 25 years, strongly advocate the use of a light racket with a small handle, to allow some flexibility of the wrist.

SAFETY FACTORS

1. Be aware from the beginning of the dangers of wild swinging of rackets with four players in a confined space.
2. Try to keep your players well spaced out and warn them not to hit the ball if they are close to another player.
3. Remind them not to enter a court without first warning those who are playing on it.
4. Check that the door is properly shut and the handle not sticking out.
5. Make sure that balls are not left lying all over the court for another player to trip over.

RULES

The rules given in the introduction to the game and the section on rules and marking should help you, but be sure that you know and have access to the up to date rules, as not all are included in these notes, and there are minor changes from time to time.

LESSON SEQUENCE

Depending on the time available, the number of courts and players, and their ability, so the rate at which you can progress through these lessons will vary. You might also vary the order in which you progress through the strokes. If your players are good ball players, you could perhaps start with backhands. This gets over the mental block some people seem to have about backhand strokes, and the extra degree of turn needed for the shot may then carry over to encourage an adequate turn on the forehand side. Volleys could perhaps be introduced earlier.

The order given in these lesson plans is an orthodox progression through drives, serve, volley, angles, etc., and the following is a typical plan for a lesson which you might use.

1. Introduction or revision of previous lesson.
2. Demonstration of new stroke or practice for the lesson.
3. Let the group all try this. You may need to feed the ball to them.
4. Divide the group up to practise on the courts.
5. Incorporate what they have learned into some sort of competition or game, bringing in tactics and rules as they arise.

LESSON 1—THE FOREHAND

1. INTRODUCTION

With all your group on one court, have a quick rally with yourself, showing that you have to hit the ball onto the front wall and return the ball before it bounces twice.

Check for left handed players as you show them the grip and then distribute them round the courts to try to keep a rally going with themselves, either two playing at a time or three if they are not too wild. If the courts are cold and your group not hard hitters, it is possible to have four at a time hitting onto the side wall. Make sure that they all have a turn and suggest to those waiting that they can practise hitting the ball up, using different faces of the racket, or pat the ball very gently on the wall at the back of the court.

2. DEMONSTRATION—FOREHAND DRIVE

When most of the group can contact the ball most of the time, gather them onto one court again, or demonstrate on each court in turn, pointing out the sideways stance for the forehand, the swing and that you hit the ball a comfortable distance opposite your left knee. Place the group opposite you along the side wall to see this and then behind you so that they are in the same position as you. This is shown in Figures 28 and 29.

3. PRACTICE

Divide the group up again to practise hitting forehands to themselves, and go around helping individually.

Figs. 28 and 29. Positions on the court to demonstrate forehands

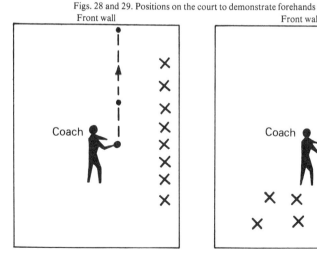
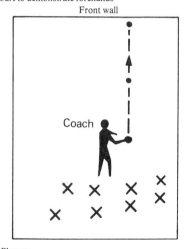

X . . . Players

Figs. 30 and 31. Positions on the court to feed forehands

4. FEEDING

You may have to feed the ball for them each to hit in turns if they cannot get a rally going.

It is easier to begin with, for your players, if you can feed the ball to them in the position shown in Figure 30. This makes it possible for your players to step into the shot and ensures that the ball is not coming in towards them. However, it is difficult to spot faults when the players are in this position, so it is a good idea also to feed the ball from behind the player, so that they get used to watching the ball being hit from behind them and aiming to get the ball straight to the back of the court, as shown in Figure 31.

It is essential to be able to place the ball so that it hits the front wall and comes back to bounce on the floor and into a position where a beginner can hit it easily. Correct any faults that are obviously hindering a player, but remember that the important thing at this stage is for them to learn by practice to hit the ball and keep a rally going.

Some of your group may need to get very close to the wall and just pat the ball onto it, starting with the ball very near or even on the racket.

Re-demonstrate if necessary, and with boys you will find that it helps to point out that the forehand shot is the same action as throwing a ball straight at the front wall, keeping it low to hit just above the tin. Girls often cannot throw anyway so this is little help to them and you may have to accept a rather wider arm swing and less of a throwing action from some of them.

Make sure this is not so wide as to be really dangerous. Remind them that it is not like a tennis swing.

5. COMPETITIONS

Some possible competitions you can introduce at this stage are as follows:

(*a*) Counting shots in a one person rally.
(*b*) Team rally with each player hitting the ball in turn. You may need to hit the shot after each player in turn to keep this going.
(*c*) Pairs rally, starting with a forehand drive and trying to keep a rally going with a partner. At the end of the rally, the winner scores one point and the loser changes with another player. Any player scoring three points running also changes with another player.
(*d*) Mini-game, starting with a forehand across to the other player and played up to five points. Explain scoring with service, out of court markings and other elementary points about the game, leaving out the service rules.

LESSON 2—THE BACKHAND

1. REVISION

Divide the group onto the courts to practise the forehand in twos or threes. Go around checking the obvious faults in the grip, position relative to the ball and the swing, giving a further demonstration of the stroke.

2. DEMONSTRATION—BACKHAND DRIVE

With the whole group on one court, show the backhand, having a rally with yourself to emphasise the sideways stance with a greater turn away, the swing, and the positioning to hit the ball opposite the front knee.

3. PRACTICE

Divide them up to practise in twos. You will probably need to do quite a lot of feeding for this shot, using the same position as for the forehand, but on the other side of the court. Some of your players may be able to drop and hit the ball, throw it up to bounce on the floor and then hit it, or throw onto the side wall to bounce on the floor and then hit. When they can keep a backhand rally going, they may still have to start it off with a forehand. Players who are waiting, or who cannot make contact, can practise hitting the ball up on the backhand face of the racket and then try to hit it gently onto the wall at the back of the court.

4. COMPETITIONS

These will be the same as in lesson one on the forehand. Emphasise the elementary tactics in the game, of hitting the ball away from the opponent and getting quickly back to the middle of the court (this is roughly where the short and half court lines meet, usually called the 'T'). Try to get them to use the straight length shot to get the ball to the back of the court. A good length shot is one which takes its second bounce near the back wall, but obviously the position of the first bounce will depend on the height and power of the shot and the speed of the ball. This is a good time to point out how they can vary the length of the shot by hitting it higher or lower on the front wall. Introduce the rules as the situations arise on the court but to begin with make sure that they have a 'let' and replay the rally if there is any danger of hitting their opponent with the racket or the ball.

LESSON 3—THE SERVICE AND ITS RETURN

1. REVISION

Start with the practices for backhands and forehands used in previous lessons. As your players improve they will be able to hit alternate shots in pairs along each side wall. Check any bad faults and re-demonstrate if necessary. If most of your group can make contact with a ball thrown from the other hand, you can start on the service.

2. DEMONSTRATION

With the whole group on one court, introduce the service, showing that you start with one foot inside the lines of the service box, that the ball is hit without bouncing it on the ground first, must touch the front wall (before any other wall) above the 'cut' line and land (if not volleyed) in the opposite back quarter of the court. It is easier for the players to see if you demonstrate initially from the left hand service box, but explain that it is usual against a right handed player to take the first service from the right hand box, so that it goes to the opponent's backhand.

Demonstrate both the high lob serve and a harder serve which can be hit overarm, as some of your players may find one type easier than another. Emphasise hitting the underside of the ball, to get height with the lob serve.

Where the service goes is more important than how it is hit, so show that the high lob hits the front wall near the out of court line a little past the middle, aiming to touch the opposite side wall high up level with the back of the service box, then drops to the floor near the back of the court.

The harder serve hits the front wall just above the 'cut' line, a little past the middle, then the opposite side wall low down near the back of the service box and takes its second bounce on the floor near the back wall.

Show that you would move to the middle of the court after the serve and demonstrate the standard return of serve straight down the nearest side wall, either as a drive or a volley.

Explain the service rules for the elementary game, and where to stand to receive service.

3. PRACTICE

Divide the group onto the courts, with two players serving at a time from opposite service boxes. Change them over with the other pair when they have had about six serves. Make sure they have tried the serve from each service box.

Any players who are still struggling to make contact with the ball can practise from closer to the front wall, starting with the ball almost touching the racket. After a while they should be able to move gradually further away from the front wall and eventually back to the service box.

Then try having one player serving and another receiving the serve and trying to hit a straight shot which lands in their own quarter of the court. Rotate this round, so that each player has tried the service and the return from both sides of the court.

4. COMPETITIONS

(a) Counting the number of correct serves out of six for each player.
(b) Each player has six serves and six returns from both sides of the court. The server scores one point for a correct serve and the receiver scores one point for a return which lands in their own quarter of the court, or for a serve which is out of court.
(c) Mini games with a correct serve. It may be necessary to bend the service rules so that the second serve is always played even if it is a fault and the ball may be bounced on the ground first, if that is the only way a player can get it into play. Explain the marker's call of 'Hand-Out' when the service changes hands. The server's score should always be called first.

LESSON 4—THE VOLLEY

1. REVISION

Practise straight drives and service.

2. DEMONSTRATION

Introduce the volley, hitting the ball before it reaches the floor, which is essential for the return of a good serve and to speed up the game, giving your opponent less time for his shot. Demonstrate the length volley played from a straight high shot and then from a serve, both backhand and forehand.

Emphasise the early backswing, sideways stance and the follow through towards the spot where the ball is aimed, which should be above the 'cut' line.

3. PRACTICES

(a) With one player on each side of the court, hitting a high shot and trying to volley it back. You will probably have to feed some of this yourself.

(b) One player serves and the other tries to volley the ball to a length down the side wall.

If some of your players have trouble with this shot, it may help to first of all get them to just stop the ball with the racket, then stop and push it, then play the full stroke.

4. COMPETITIONS

Play full games up to nine points, with one of the spare players keeping the score.

Explain what happens if they get to 8–8 and the receiver has the option of 'set two' so that the game finishes at ten points or 'no set', with the game finishing at the usual nine points.

If your players seem unwilling to use the newly practised volley in the game, try putting a bonus point on any rally which is won with a volley.

This system can be used when any new shot has been introduced, to encourage its use in the game.

LESSON 5—ANGLES

1. REVISION

Practise straight drives, service and volley returns.

2. DEMONSTRATION

Explain the value of an angle as an attacking shot to get the ball quickly to the opposite front corner of the court when your opponent is behind you on the same side of the court. Also explain its use to return a ball that has gone too far past you or too deep into the corner for a straight shot to be played. Demonstrate by first throwing the ball onto the nearest side wall, behind the 'short' line and then playing an angle shot to reach the opposite front corner.

Show the same shot played on the backhand, and then the forehand and backhand angle played from a straight drive. Emphasise hitting the ball later and with more turn on the backswing.

3. PRACTICES

(a) With one player on each side of the court, they can throw the ball onto the nearest side wall, to bounce on the floor and then play their angle shot. Make sure they try from each side and change round with the other pair.

(b) Then get them to play an angle from a straight drive hit by themselves or another player. You will probably have to feed some of this yourself, particularly on the backhand side. Rotate the players round so that you feed the shot to each in turn.

4. COMPETITIONS

You will have been introducing the rules as the need for them arose in the game, but be sure that your players know the service rules and the rules concerned with hitting the player with the ball.

As this may well be the week before half term, you might try an American type tournament on the all play all basis, keeping the total points score, and not the option to 'set two' at 8–8, as this can distort the points score. Have a scorer for each match.

FURTHER PROGRESS

Apart from improving the technique of the shots, there are a number of things you can add into the teaching programme.

1. Try some of the more difficult practices included in the section on technique.
2. Teach some more shots to get greater variety in the game, using cross court length shots, boast (this is a side wall shot played to return a ball from deep in the back corners), lobs, drop shots, short volleys and a short hard kill into the 'nick'. These are all described in the Technique section, and can be introduced in the same way as the basic shots.
3. Arrange a good demonstration for your group to watch or take them to a tournament which is being played locally. The SRA and the WSRA can supply information about these. When watching a top class game of squash, try to give some kind of commentary on the action to show your group the tactics being used and the shots which are most effective.
4. Work for the Proficiency Certificate set jointly by the two associations. A copy of the requirements for these is included in the Appendix at the end of these notes.
5. It may be possible to arrange a match against another school, or enter some of your players for a Junior tournament. Most squash clubs have a Junior section which some of the more enthusiastic might like to join.

Tactics in Match Play

The elementary tactics (elementary is probably the wrong word, as they remain difficult to apply at any level) have been described already, but need to be emphasised again, as they are important at any standard of play. You will often see International players muttering to themselves on court, and as well as some things that may be better left unheard, they are probably telling themselves to—'watch the ball' . . . 'hit it away from him, not back to him' . . . 'move quicker back to the "T"' . . . 'hit it straight, not across the court where he keeps cutting it off' . . . . The basis of the game is to play the length shot parallel and close to the side wall or wide across the court, to keep your opponent pinned in the back corners.

However, although this may force your opponent to play defensively and he may play a weak return which you can attack, you will need to do more than this to move him round the court, so that he has to work much harder and stretch to reach your shots. Thinking is the all-important factor here, for you should always have a reason for every shot you play, even if it is only what shot to play to get yourself out of trouble. A poor stroke played to the best place may often be more effective than a superb one played straight back to your opponent.

Before considering which shot to play in a rally during the game, you need some information about the court you have to play on, your opponent and yourself.

THE COURT

The temperature of the court makes a lot of difference as the warmer it is, the faster the ball will travel, and the higher it will bounce. It is very hard to play winners on a hot court and the rallies will go on much longer, which is a great test of your stamina. You will need to be very patient, and play accurate controlled squash, moving your opponent round the court until he is far enough out of position for a winning shot to be possible. When the ball is flying about very fast, it is probably more effective to get the ball into the front of the court with an angle shot, than to try to play a delicate drop shot. The playing height of the court is something you need to look at, as some courts have beams or ceilings which are so low that high lob shots are impossible to play and you will need to think of some other way of getting the ball into the back corners if you normally use a lob or a lob serve. Some courts, on the other hand, may have rather dazzling lights which cause a ball lobbed high into the air to turn into just one of a series of black spots in front of the eyes. Floors can be another hazard, if they are very dark or shiny, as this makes it difficult to sight a low, hard shot, or causes it to skid. The joint between the side walls and the floor may be unusually large, giving you a greater chance than normal of hitting this 'nick' when you aim for it. On cold courts, even rather poor shots may turn into winners if you are careful to play the ball as far away as possible from your opponent, and it is worth going for your winner as soon as it is at all reasonable.

Probably the most difficult court to play on is the 'sweating' one, where the walls and at worst the floor as well are dripping wet from condensation. This causes the ball to skid, making wide angle shots come out into the middle of the court and high lobs go through the roof. Your game on this kind of court has to be reduced to hard length shots, including the serve, played to touch the side wall near the service box, as they will then skid along the side wall and be very difficult to play. A very narrow angle still works well and so do short cut shots. If the floors are very wet as well, you might as well be playing on the local skating rink and would be well advised to cancel the game.

YOUR OPPONENT

You may have heard something about your opponent, or played him before, so that you have some idea of the sort of game he plays and perhaps even the sort of game that he does not like. He will have his own favourite shots and perhaps a particularly weak shot that you can attack. In any case you may be able to find out some of these things in the knock up, which can help you to decide what sort of game to play in the beginning. If it becomes obvious that your original plan of action is not effective, you should not hesitate to change it, perhaps trying a spell of slow balling, when your fast attacking shots are all being returned even faster.

It is generally assumed that tall people can cut off high shots very easily, but have more trouble getting down to low ones and in turning quickly. Therefore, the hard shot hit low and wide will probably be the most effective, combined with attempts to deceive them into going the wrong way. Shorter players tend to be rather quicker to turn, but having a shorter reach, can be passed more easily across the court and in the air. Older players may have a lot of skill and experience, but are likely to lack stamina, so it pays to keep up the pressure and return the ball at all costs in the hope that they will eventually run out of steam. The younger player may lack experience and be more easily confused by deceptive play, but is likely to have speed and stamina. These rather wild generalisations can be easily disproved by particular individuals, but they do at least give you something to start on in deciding your general tactics.

Make sure you notice if your opponent is left handed, as this can be a problem, particularly if you tend to plug away constantly at the back left hand corner of the court. It may be better to switch your attack to his backhand, but you cannot assume that it will be the weaker shot. The left handed player is harder to read, so you will need to watch him carefully.

YOURSELF

Your own state of fitness may be a factor in deciding tactics, because if you feel that your stamina is poor, it is pointless to get involved in too many long rallies, so you will have to take more chances than usual and go for accurate shots to finish the rally off more quickly.

No discussion of tactics in match play could be complete without some mention of fitness training. Many players start to play squash to keep fit, but when their standard reaches a certain level, they find that they have to get fit to play squash.

There are many possible programmes to increase speed, build up strength and improve stamina, but most of them include the following activities:

1. Skipping to speed up footwork.
2. Track or cross country running for stamina.
3. Shuttle running or potato races for speed. Turning and bending over short distances.
4. Interval running—short sprints for various distances to improve your speed.
5. Exercises (possibly using weights) in a circuit to strengthen arms, legs, back and abdominal muscles.
6. Shadow playing on the court, running to each corner and back to the 'T' for a fixed time with fixed rest intervals.

This type of programme has to be carfully worked out so that it is within the player's capacity and carefully progressed.

Having sorted out your own fitness, there are quite a number of tactical moves which you can consider in the knock up, service and service return, before the game gets really under way.

THE KNOCK UP

The rules allow five minutes before a match to knock up with your opponent, giving you two and a half minutes on the forehand side and the same on the backhand. During that time, you will be studying your opponent, getting your own shots working, your eyes used to the court lights, assessing the pace the ball will play at and getting yourself and the ball warm. Move around during the knock up, so that you play some shots from near the front of the court and others from further back. Send your opponent a variety of shots, to see how he copes with them. Although you do not want to hog the ball, it is a good idea to hit a straight shot sometimes, because this is after all the shot you will want to use most often during the game, rather than the cross court shot. Most essential is to make sure that you can hit a good length.

SERVICE AND SERVICE RETURN

Tactical points about the serve and service return have already been
discussed in the section on technique, but there are a few more that
can be considered:

1. Although it is usual to serve to the opponent's backhand initially,
   if they frequently play winners or particularly good returns from
   this side, it is better to start serving to their forehand side.
2. It can be disconcerting to your opponent if you switch to serving
   on to their forehand, so this is a tactical move you might consider.
3. You may well find it more effective to use a hard length serve
   down the middle or straight at your opponent, if they are very
   good at playing an attacking volley from the serve going to the
   side wall.
4. The usual position to receive serve is about a foot behind the back
   corner of the service box but you may have to adjust this forward
   or back to be able to cope more effectively with your opponent's
   serve. You may be able to attack the serve by standing further
   forward. The most important thing to remember when returning
   the serve is to concentrate (particularly when your opponent is
   serving well) on playing a safe return. This usually means a high
   straight length shot, or possibly a high cross court lob.
5. If you find that your opponent is moving forward to attack your
   serve, you will have to vary the serve to make it hit the side wall
   nearer the front of the court.
6. The high lob serve is little use if the walls are wet as it will tend to
   skid up and out of court. It is also little use if your opponent is one
   of those fortunate people who can pick even the best serve out of
   the rafters and volley it dead into the front corner. In all these
   circumstances, as well as on a court with low beams or ceiling,
   you will need to use your hard length serve.

WHAT SHOT TO PLAY?

If you have a choice and are not just desperately trying to return the
ball, then you must have some idea what you want to do when the
rally is in progress. Your basic tactics tell you to hit the ball away

Figs. 32–33. What shot to play?

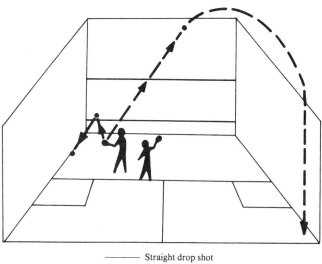

——— Straight drop shot
------ Cross court lob

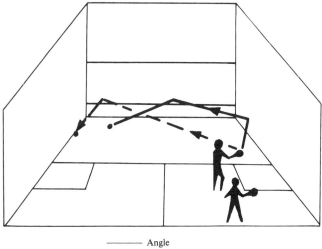

——— Angle
------ Cross court drop

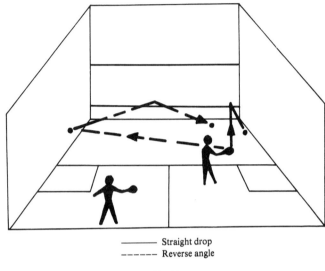

—————— Straight drop
– – – – – – Reverse angle

Fig. 34

from your opponent but first of all you have to know where he is. This is easy enough if he is in front of you, but when your opponent is behind you on the court, this is rather more difficult. It may be possible to see him out of the corner of your eye as you move in to play your shot, or you may hear him as he thunders up the court, but you will often have to judge his position by knowing where he started from and where he is most likely to move to. The last shot you played tells you his starting position, and if he has only just reached it at full stretch, he will have little time to regain a good position, so you should obviously play the next shot to the diagonally opposite corner.

If you have played the same shot in the same situation several times before, your opponent will begin to anticipate this and move towards it, giving you a good opportunity for a winner with a shot in the diagonally opposite corner. Figure 32 shows a typical situation, where the player, having played the ball into the front backhand corner, is now expecting your drop shot and beginning to move up behind you, so that he will be badly out of position for a cross court lob. Figures 33 and 34 show the obvious shots to play when your opponent is behind you at the back of the court. When he is on your side of the court, you have the choice of an angle or a cross court drop, the angle being the most used, as the drop shot is much slower, giving your opponent more time to reach it. With your opponent on the other side of the court, you have the choice of a straight drop or the reverse angle.

Your choice of shot may be governed by your assessment of the court, your opponent and the type of game he dislikes, or some other factor. There is not much point in playing the ball to a position where your opponent plays his most lethal shot, so you will have to try to organise the rally to keep away from that spot. Your own position on the court may dictate the best shot, if for instance you have been forced near the front of the court at full stretch to reach a short ball, unless you play a certain winner, it is usually a good idea to play a high slow ball to give yourself time to get back in position again. Inexperienced players tend, on the whole, to go for winners before they are reasonably possible, either trying to play a winning shot from a really difficult return, or when their opponent is in a commanding position in the middle of the court. Trying to play winners from the back of the court is usually a disaster. Wait until your opponent is behind you and has played a poor length shot before you go for the winner at the front of the court. At the beginning of a game, it is better to play fairly steadily until your game is working well, and at any time you have to work your opponent out of position before going for the winning shot. When in doubt or difficulty, it is usually best to fall back on the length shot close to the side wall.

ANTICIPATION

To give yourself more time to play a good shot, or even at times to reach it at all, it is essential to anticipate where your opponent's shot is going to go. Although there are eight possible shots that can be played from most positions on the court, some are more likely than others and from some positions there are only one or two shots that can be played. A good length shot, if it is not cut off on the volley before it reaches the back of the court can probably only be returned with a boast to the opposite front corner. This means that you can start moving in that direction, keeping an eye on the ball in case it comes further off the back wall than you expected, allowing your opponent to hit it straight.

With increasing experience, you learn to pick up small cues from a player's position or way of hitting the ball which will show you what he is going to do. It may be that you have seen him play before and know that he has a favourite shot from a certain position, or that there are some shots which he rarely attempts to play.

DECEPTION

To make it more difficult for your opponent to anticipate your shot, or to get him going the wrong way, you need to be able to disguise your intention. The stroke should look the same whether you are going to hit hard or soft, high or low, straight, across court or into the side wall. The racket head can be slowed at the last minute to change an apparent bullet into a soft drop shot, or an apparent drop can be suddenly lifted high on to the front wall for a cross court lob. The same stroke can contact the ball earlier for the cross court, or later for the angle into the side wall and at the front of the court, variation and deception can be achieved by angling or pulling across court an apparent straight drop. It is more unsettling for your opponent if you vary the pace of your game, so that he cannot get into a rhythm.

CONCENTRATION

Though not really a tactic, concentration is essential in match play, and has to be maintained in the face of possibly dubious decisions by the marker or referee, your own poor play, or your opponent's lucky shots. Whatever happens, you must concentrate only on what you are trying to do to win a game.

Some Landmarks in the History of Squash Rackets

1800s

Actual facts about the origins of squash as a game are hard to find, but it seems to have evolved as a practice game for the racket players at Harrow around the middle 1800s. The story goes that a soft ball was used, so that expensive rackets balls were not wasted and, perhaps more important, the school windows were not broken. Lord Dunedin is quoted by Susan Noel (1948) as saying that when he was at Harrow in 1863, the game was played in different yards of the boarding houses wherever three walls occurred in a suitable position. It was known to have been played for a long time, and the favourite spot was known as 'the corner', but after 1865, some rugby fives courts were also used. The name 'squash' is thought to come from the noise made as the ball—a soft rubber one, often with a hole made in it to slow it down—hit the wall.

The first known purpose-built court was constructed by a former Harrovian, Vernon Harcourt, at his home in Oxford. This court was six feet longer than the present standard of thirty-two feet but had the same width at twenty-one feet. The play line on the front wall was thirty inches, compared with the nineteen inches of the modern court. Many more courts were built in the late 1800s, in private houses, public schools and London social clubs, but although rules were laid down in 1886 and squash recognised as a separate game, there were no standard measurements and courts were of many different sizes. Neither was there any standard ball, each club playing with their own favourite missile, but all of them being probably much faster than the present ball. The then Prince of Wales was a keen player and this gave a great boost in popularity to the game.

EARLY 1900s

In the early 1900s many courts were built in the US and in 1906 they held the first ever National Championships. The court measurements ($2\frac{1}{2}$ feet narrower) and rules standardised by the US SRA in 1907 were different to those later standardised by most other countries. This has, over the years, made International competition with the US something of a problem, although a British men's team played with considerable success in the US in 1924 and 1926. The British women played a regular biennial match for the Wolfe-Noel cup, against the US from 1933 until 1963, when fixtures began to be arranged with Australia, South Africa and New Zealand, all of whom play our type of game.

Although the SRA was not formed in this country until 1928, standard measurements were laid down in 1911 by the sub-committee of the Tennis (real Tennis) and Rackets Association which administered the game. The measurements chosen were those of the Bath Club court, as this happened to be the club used by most of the top officials of that time.

The game at this time was played almost entirely by men who had started as Rackets players and therefore tended to play a hard hitting game of heavily cut shots, played short or to a length. The first true squash player was said to be J. E. Palmer-Tomkinson who dominated the game until the middle 1920s.

1922–23 marked the start of men's and women's championships and the Public Schools event (Evans Cup) for boys under 19 and under 16. The under 19 section rather faded away, because of the greater popularity of the Drysdale Cup which started in 1925 and featured many players who later reached international level.

The inaugural meeting of the SRA in 1928 marked a significant step in the growth of the game, and by 1939 when the war halted development, the original 25 clubs which had affiliated to the SRA in 1929 had grown to 146. The women set up a separate Association in 1934 which continues to manage their affairs.

POST WAR

The war caused a considerable setback in the growth of the game, as many courts were destroyed and building restrictions prevented any court construction until the middle 1950s.

The decade from 1950 was dominated by two players, Hashim Khan and Janet Morgan. With his brother, Azam, and cousin, Roshan, Hashim was in a different class from other players of the time, with his speed and retrieving ability, plus accuracy of shot. He is generally credited with the introduction of the crash kill into the side wall/floor 'nick' which became a feature of modern squash.

Unbeaten from the time that she first won the British Championships in 1949 until her retirement in 1959, Janet Morgan (Shardlow) has continued to exert a strong influence on the game through her services to the WSRA. Janet is the only player to have held all three titles, British, US and Australian.

The great spurt in court building which took place in Australia in the later 1950s, brought their players into the forefront of International squash by 1961, when Heather McKay started her reign as the World's No. 1 player. With a rare blend of talents, Heather is not only a superb stroke player, but has great concentration, tactical skill and the ability to play better with increasing pressure. All this, combined with tremendous application to the job of continually improving her game, has ensured that she has remained unbeaten to the present day (1975).

The following year (1962) saw the British men's team beaten by the Australians, and their leading player, Ken Hiscoe, also won the Amateur Championships.

However, the early 1960s also saw a considerable expansion in growth in this country, with courts increasing at a rate of over 8% per annum. These were largely at Members' clubs, in contrast to Australia, where the expansion was largely in proprietary and municipal courts.

1966 marked a turning point in this country with the return of a British player to the top ranks. Jonah Barrington won the Amateur title in 1966, held it until he turned Professional two years later and was the first British player to hold the Open title as well as the Amateur.

Commercial interests became involved in the building of squash courts in the late 1960s and this, together with the growth of Sports Centres, has led in the last seven years to an enormous expansion of the game.

The rate of increase in individual members of the SRA has been 14% per annum since 1962. The WSRA have recorded an even greater increase in members, with 19% per annum. The sale of rackets too has been increasing by 18% per annum since 1962.

Apart from swimming, squash now rates as the most popular activity in Sports Centres and though no accurate figures exist, Alan Jenkins (1973) suggests that there were about 360,000 participants in 1972.

Sponsors have been coming more and more into the game in the last few years, providing gradually increasing prizes for tournaments and staged matches. This has been considerably aided by the introduction of glass back walls, which have been fitted to a number of Championship courts, making it possible for larger galleries to be built, where all the spectators get a good view of the game.

There seems no reason to suppose that the recent growth rate should not continue for a good many years, and squash will no doubt come to hold a far more important place in the Physical Education syllabus of schools and colleges.

Appendix 'A'

REQUIREMENTS FOR THE JUNIOR PROFICIENCY CERTIFICATE FOR BOYS AND GIRLS UNDER 19 YEARS

ELEMENTARY

1. To serve correctly 4 services out of 6 attempts from each box where the ball, when served, hits the opposite side wall behind the short line and bounces in the correct back quarter of the court.
2. To drive directly onto the front wall off a simple service, so that the ball returns and bounces behind the short line. The ball to be returned by the candidate on her side of the court (i.e. parallel to side wall) 4 attempts out of 6, to be correct on both forehand and backhand.
3. To play 4 out of 6 side wall shots, forehand and backhand, from the service box area so that the ball bounces near the front corner on the opposite side of the court and is not higher on the front wall than the 'cut' line. The ball to be fed by the Examiner so that it returns to the candidate reasonably parallel to the side wall.
4. To play a game, showing the ability to serve correctly, including 8-all (orally, if necessary), and understand the positions of server and receiver for each rally.

INTERMEDIATE

1. As above, but the service must bounce behind the service box in the correct back quarter of the court.
2. As above, but the ball must be returned not only to bounce behind the short line, but also no further from the side wall than the width of the service box.

3. As above, but the Examiner to feed the ball so that the candidate plays it off the side wall.

4. The volley, both forehand and backhand, 4 out of 6 attempts correctly so that the ball hits the front wall and returns parallel to the side wall. The candidate to stand on the short line.

5. To play a game to show understanding of hitting the ball away from the opponent and being able to get to the centre of the court after every ball hit. If not already taken Elementary stage, then also as in 4.

ADVANCED

1. 1 and 2 as Elementary, but 8 out of 10 correct.

3. To boast 4 out of 6 balls out of both back corners to get to the front wall so that the ball bounces near the front opposite corner. Examiner to feed the ball onto back side wall first, then back wall, about 3 feet high.

4. To return 4 out of 6 services correctly so that the ball is returned parallel to the side wall, bouncing behind the short line and not further away than the width of the service box; or as a boast to the opposite front corner and below cut line.

5. To play a game to show tactics as in Intermediate level, and also to watch the opponent play the ball. Also to show appreciation of the need to allow the opponent to move directly to the ball and play to any part of the front wall.

Appendix 'B'

MAIN AIMS

The training of coaches to teach at beginner level only, in both a GROUP and INDIVIDUAL LESSON.

STANDARD REQUIRED OF APPLICANTS TO ATTEND COURSE

Candidates should be of adequate club standard and should be able to give a reasonable demonstration of FOREHAND, BACKHAND, SERVICE, VOLLEY, SIDE WALL SHOTS, BACK CORNER SHOTS, LOB AND DROPSHOT (only need to demonstrate in a static situation for Back corner Shots, Lob and Dropshot). They should be capable of feeding for these shots in practice and in the game situation. They should also be acquainted with the rules of the game and general match tactics, and be capable of marking a game.

COURSE CONTENT

Students should be given the basic techniques and teaching points of FOREHAND, BACKHAND, SERVICE, VOLLEY, SIDE WALL SHOTS, LOBS and DROPSHOTS.

The following points should be covered:

(*a*) Grip
(*b*) General positioning and positioning of body in relation to the ball

(*c*) Footwork
(*d*) Swing of racket
(*e*) Control of racket face
(*f*) Balance

Teaching Sequence for a Group or Individual Lesson

Warm-up or recap period
Demonstration and explanation of shot to be taught
Practice of shot
Activity of group or individual in game or competitive situation
Summary of lesson having achieved some success

The Elementary Course demands SIMPLE TEACHING, therefore

(*a*) Appeal through the eye before the ear when teaching
(*b*) Use simple clear demonstration, introducing the language
(*c*) Show the whole stroke first before breaking it down
(*d*) Pupils should NOT be given too much to think about at any one time

OBSERVATION, DIAGNOSIS AND CORRECTION OF FAULTS

Students will be given guidance on how to spot faults.
The fundamentals of good analysis are as follows:

(*a*) Watching the ball
(*b*) Positioning body well in relation to the ball
(*c*) Footwork
(*d*) Control of the racket face and racket swing
(*e*) Grip

Note: Inability to hit the ball—students should be given a knowledge of variety of feeding methods and ball sense activities.

TACTICS

Basic tactics should be known, as follows:

(*a*) The 'T' is the commanding position on the court

(*b*) Watch the ball at all times, especially when it is behind you

(*c*) Play the ball away from opponent and away from the middle of the court

(*d*) The value of length

(*e*) The importance of a good return of service

(*f*) Variation of pace

(*g*) Winners played from the front of the court

ORGANISATION OF GROUP AND INDIVIDUAL LESSONS

1. GROUP

Group lessons should have ACTIVITY, PURPOSE, ENJOYMENT.
When planning the session remember the following points:

1. the number of courts available
2. the number in the class
3. the ability of the class
4. the time available
5. practice of the strokes and combination of the strokes, with or without competition.

It is essential to (*a*) Have a sound technical knowledge

(*b*) Plan the content of the session

(*c*) Remember that pupils have come to learn the game, therefore

(*d*) Start a game as soon as possible

(*e*) Encourage and praise pupils when appropriate and offer constructive criticism when necessary

ENSURE THAT:

1. A clear task is given for each activity
2. All the space is being used
3. Every member of the group can see the coach and has room to swing the racket
4. *Safety measures are of the utmost importance*

5. The side as well as the front is used for demonstration and observation
6. All members of the group are involved most of the time

Group practices, relevant to the game, should be shown on all the strokes so that students have a good knowledge of group activity.

2. INDIVIDUAL LESSON

1. Introduction—find out playing background of pupil
2. Knock up with pupil—first of all trying to rally with the pupil and then, if possible, play a few points with pupil, thereby assessing the standard of the pupil
3. Having assessed the standard, select coaching point, progress to the teaching sequence.

THE TEACHING SEQUENCE

Understand the teaching sequence of both Individual and Group Lessons including practices for the shots being taught and the feeding progressions for each shot.

Students should be given guidance on course planning, and a demonstration lesson.

TALK ON ETIQUETTE

Coaches and teachers at schools are responsible for good behaviour which must start at beginner level, i.e. attitude to opponent and marker/referee.

TALK ON ESSENTIALS

1. Care of equipment
2. Choice of equipment
3. Good turnout which should be predominantly white
4. Clean, white soled shoes

TALK ON RULES

This should cover:

(a) The role of marker and referee
(b) How to score
(c) General rules, relating to fault serves, etc.
(d) Freedom of stroke and fair view of ball
(e) Difference between lets and points
(f) Hitting opponent with the ball

SECTIONS OF EXAMINATION

This will be held some time after completion of the course in order to allow practical experience in coaching.

1. Practical Test in Group Coaching

Candidates to be asked to:

(a) Introduce and demonstrate a stroke (at beginner level) and teach stroke technique, showing diagnosis and correction of faults.
(b) Show progression to group practice or game situation.

2. Practical Test in Individual Coaching

As group examination. The aim is to examine more closely actual stroke technique being coached and the student's ability to feed adequately in an individual lesson.

3. Written Test on Rules, Tactics and Techniques

Set papers to be given to candidates, which will include a major question on planning a course of group coaching.

Books and Material

SRA Publications—available from the Squash Rackets Association, 70 Brompton Road, London SW3 1DX
Note: prices are subject to change and include postage in Great Britain but not overseas.

1. *General*

SRA Handbook, published yearly	£1.00
	(free to members)
Rules of the Singles Game	
in leaflet form	25p
in wall chart form suitable for mounting	70p
The Case for Squash: its growth, develop-	
ment and prospects	£4.00 (£5 overseas)
Badges	60p + SAE

2. *Coaching*

SRA Junior Proficiency Certificates	15p
SRA Junior Development Scheme	15p
Syllabus for the Introductory One Day	
Teachers Course	15p
SRA Elementary Coaches Certificate	15p
SRA Certificate for Qualified Markers	
and Referees	15p
SRA National Development Plan	15p
Published by EP Group of Companies:	
Know the Game, Play the Game—Squash	
Rackets	30p
Squash Rackets, by Anthony Swift	£2.00 + 10p P & P

Colour Films obtainable from the production company, Gerard Holdsworth Productions Ltd., 31 Palace Street, London SW1E 5HW. Four 16 mm coaching films:

for hire per film	from £3.74 per day	Plus
for purchase per film	from £55.44	VAT

Notes of the above films are also obtainable   10p

WSRA publications—available from the WSRA, 345 Upper Richmond Road West, Sheen, London SW14 8QN
A Guide to Group Coaching, by Penny Goodall
Play and Coach Squash, by Betty Keenan

Books on Squash obtainable from the publishers (some of the earlier editions may now be out of print)
Squash Rackets for Women, by Janet Morgan (1953) Sporting Handbooks.
Squash Rackets, by Fred Brundle (1955), W. & G. Foyle Ltd
Tackle Squash Rackets This Way, by B. C. Phillips (1960), Stanley Paul
Squash Rackets, by J. H. Giles (1961), Nicholas Kaye
New Angles on Squash, by R. B. Hawkey (1962), Faber and Faber
Your Book of Squash, by R. B. Hawkey (1964), Faber and Faber
Improving your Squash, by R. B. Hawkey (1967), Faber and Faber
 Beginner's Guide to Squash, by R. B. Hawkey (1973), Pelham Books
Newer Angles on Squash, by R. B. Hawkey (1974), Faber and Faber
Squash Rackets, by R. B. Hawkey (1975), Pelham Books
Squash Rackets—The Khan Game, by Hashim Khan (1968), Souvenir Press
Squash Rackets, by Henry MacIntosh (1968), Pelham Books
Teach Yourself Squash Rackets, by Hamer and Bellamy (1968), English Universities Press
Dardir on Squash, by Dardir and Gilmour (1971), Gilmour Associates, New Zealand

The Book of Squash, by Peter Wood (1972), Van Nostrand Reinhold Co, New York

The Book of Jonah, by J. Barrington with Clive Everton (1972), Stanley Paul

Barrington on Squash, by Jonah Barrington (1973), Stanley Paul

Geoff Hunt on Squash, by Geoff Hunt (1974), Cassell

Play Better Squash, by John Beddington (1974), Queen Anne Press